Easter at Our House

Easter at Our House

Written and Illustrated by P. K. Hallinan

ideals children's books.
Nashville, Tennessee

ISBN 10: 0-8249-5552-8
ISBN 13: 978-0-8249-5552-6

Published by Ideals Children's Books
An imprint of Ideals Publications
A Guideposts Company
535 Metroplex Drive, Suite 250
Nashville, Tennessee 37211
www.idealspublications.com

Color separations by Precision Color Graphics,
Franklin, Wisconsin

Printed and bound in Italy by LEGO

Library of Congress CIP data on file

10 9 8 7 6 5 4 3 2 1

Designed by Georgina Chidlow-Rucker

This Book
Belongs to

_____

It's Easter at our house,
And oh, what a dawn,

As God pours His glory
Over garden and lawn!

We hop out of bed and race down the stairs
To scout out the candies and the Easter eggs there.

But there's no time to lose, as we plan our big search,
'Cause we want to make certain, we're not late for church.
So we hurry to look in each cranny and nook!

We spot the first egg by the fireplace bricks.
The second we find in the dry kindling sticks.

But all of a sudden, we find Easter eggs galore,
Spotting four, maybe more, on the floor by the door!

Soon, we are joined by our parents, who hold
Two beautiful baskets that are shining like gold!

And we squeal with delight, clapping and spinning—
But Easter at our house is only beginning!

We run to the kitchen for a very light meal.

We zoom to our rooms with the greatest of zeal.

And we dress up for church, just as quickly as that!
I snap my suspenders . . .

Sister pats her new hat!

The next thing you know we're all on our way,
Heading down to the park where our church meets today.

And the flowers adorn
This warm Easter morn.

The park is abounding with great sights and sounds.
Some people are talking, others walking around.

So we take a nice space at the base of a tree,
Then set up our chairs so it's easy to see.

The service begins with some wonderful songs.
The worship team leads, and we all sing along.

Then Pastor Sinclair greets everyone there.
He offers a smile and an elegant prayer.

But next comes his sermon
About God's love so dear.
When he shouts, "Christ is risen!"
There's both cheering and tears.

Then we stand up in place,
Sing a song, and embrace.

Soon, we descend to a creek where it bends,
So folks can be baptized before family and friends.

And, oh, what elation as the pastor baptizes
All kinds of believers, in all colors and sizes!

But Easter's not over—there's still the big feast!
Our restaurant is jammed, but they find us some seats.

We kids order pancakes, with bacon on the side.
Mom opts for Cobb salad; Dad tries steak and fries.

Later that evening,
Before going to bed,
We listen in silence
As a story is read.

It's all about Easter,
And how Jesus gave
His life for us all,
So the world could be saved.

So we end up in prayer
As we kneel and we say,
"Lord, thank you for Easter . . .

"It's the greatest of days!"